MIRANDA

SMOKING HOT LESBIAN EROTICA

Drilling for a FILLING

THE LAURA AND SARA CHRONICLES

BOOK 9

WARNING

This book contains sexually explicit scenes and adult language. It may be considered offensive to some readers. This book is for sale to adults ONLY.

* * * * * * * * * * * * * * * * * * *

Please store your files wisely where they cannot be accessed by underage readers.

Please feel free to send me an email. Just know that these emails are filtered by my publisher. Good news is always welcome.

Miranda Mars - **Miranda_mars@awesomeauthors.org**

You might also want to check my blog for Updates and interesting info. http://miranda-mars.awesomeauthors.org/

About the Publisher

4Fun Publishing, a member of **BLVNP Incorporated**, 340 S. Lemon #6200, Walnut CA 91789, info@blvnp.com / legal@blvnp.com
NOTE: Due to the highly emotional reaction of some people to works of erotic fiction, any email sent to the above address that contains foul language or religious references is automatically deleted by our anti-spam software and will not be seen. All other communications are welcome.

DISCLAIMER

Please don't be stupid and kill yourself. This book is a work of FICTION. Do not try any new sexual practice that you find in this book. It is fiction and not to be confused with reality. Neither the author nor the publisher or its associates assume any responsibility for any loss, injury, death or legal consequences resulting from acting on the contents in this book. Every character in this book is over 18 years of age. The author's opinions are not to be construed as the opinions of the publisher. The material in this book is for entertainment purposes ONLY. Enjoy.

The Laura and Sara Chronicles, Book 9

Drilling for a Filling

Smoking Hot Lesbian Erotica

By: Miranda Mars

ISBN: 978-1-62761-992-9

Twice a year Laura had to get her teeth cleaned, and Sara, who still held down the fort at her dentist's office, where they had first met years earlier, with incendiary sexual and emotional consequences, made the appointments. She made them all late in the day, so that Laura would be the final patient into the office. It usually worked out that she and Laura would wind up in Sara's apartment fucking like two lust-crazed bunnies, reliving their original desire for each other, and trying to control the bittersweet memories of their lengthy intimacy that roiled through them both while their bodies were locked together in seizures of heart-racing ecstasy.

So it was with some excited tingling of anticipation that Laura entered the medical/dental building at 450 Sutter and listened to her heels clicking on the smooth marble floors as she walked the echoing corridors to keep the appointment Sara had made for her.

These days, of course, both of them had to maneuver through the shoals of their permanent relationships—Sara with Darlene, her dental hygienist lover, who worked in the same building though for another dentist, and Laura with Makeeda, her wife, who was currently appearing at a jazz club in Chicago—in order to consummate these twice yearly late afternoon sessions of sexual and emotional catharsis. Laura, as she opened the fogged glass door of the dental office and stepped inside, knew that she herself was free for the evening with nothing to worry about but the vague, lingering guilt of having spent hours in bed with Sara instead of being true to Makeeda. She could feel a happy tingling in her pussy at the thought of it. But what of Darlene? Would Sara be likewise free to indulge in their biannual tryst?

Sara looked up from behind the dark polished wood counter where her desk was, flanked by huge shelves of patient files. She winked at Laura and made a modified version of one of her funny faces. They had not seen each other for six months, and Laura's heart, at least her own heart, was pinched by the sight of her just as sharply as it had been the first time, when she had realized that she had to have this woman in her arms or life would never be complete.

"Hello, Sara." (". . . darling," she breathed, silently, so that none of the other patients in the waiting room would overhear. There were only two this late in the afternoon.)

Sara was never fooled by Laura's sentimentality. She returned her affection, and her lust, but had never stopped blaming Laura for abandoning her for Makeeda. Her funny face turned pointedly, ironically sour, and she mouthed the word "Sit," indicating one of the waiting room sofas.

Laura sat and leafed idly through a two-year-old copy of *Fast Company* magazine until her name was called. Ick. How to be a winner. How to think of new ways to cripple your competitors. How to develop the killer instinct. Seventeen productive ways to spend five minutes instead of checking your email again. Maybe I have chosen the wrong life, she mused.

Finally, the other two waiting patients having disappeared, Sara called her name. They exchanged a businesslike smile as Laura passed her on the way in. "Talk to me on the way out," she murmured to Laura.

What did this mean? Was she going to cancel? Cancel what? They certainly had not said: "After I get my teeth cleaned, we can adjourn to your apartment and fuck ourselves silly." Laura was merely expecting it because they had done it so often in the past. Maybe Sara was backing out? Maybe Darlene was causing trouble? Or in some other way making it impossible for Sara?

These thoughts and feelings tormented her while the dentist was briskly inspecting and ultrasounding the plaque off her teeth. He knew that Sara and she were old friends, though he probably knew no more than that, and so was unsurprised when she lingered by Sara's desk as he was leaving.

The back office door clicked, he was gone, they were alone. Laura wasted no time in bending over and kissing Sara on the cheek, then on the neck, where she still sat at her desk. "I'm hungry for your body," she whispered. "I want to fuck you until you scream."

Sara giggled softly and squirmed away. "Cut that out! Have some manners, okay?"

"Why? He's not coming back, is he? Aren't we alone?"

Sara flirted. "Just because we're alone doesn't give you the right to—"

"To kiss you?"

"You were doing more than just kissing."

"I'm sorry," Laura feigned contrition. "Did I say something that offended you?"

"God, if you want to know the truth," Sara confessed, "I felt a little squirt of happy juice in my pussy when you said that."

"All right, then." Laura helped her up out of her office chair with one hand. "Let's get cracking. My car is parked in the Union Square garage."

But Sara's face fell. "I have bad news."

"Oh shit. You're kidding." One of Laura's downer scenarios was coming true. *Just tell me it's not that bitch Darlene.*

"My Mama," Sara said, downcast. "She's here from Mississippi." She made an exceptionally (for her) screwy face: full, pillowy lips, the lips Laura always longed to devour, pursed in a violent moue, her eyes crossed, her tongue lolling out. "She won't understand if we come home and start pearl diving in the bedroom."

Laura grabbed her and pulled her close, wrapping her tightly in her arms and fastening her lips like a sucker fish again on her pretty black neck. "Mmmm, you have the pearl I want," she panted, sucking, then nipping Sara's earlobe.

"Cut it out!" Sara laughed, wriggling free. "You just want me for my fantastic body anyway, you beast. You lecher!"

"It *is* pretty fantastic," Laura agreed.

Sara did not, actually, have a fantastic body, at least nothing to compare with the peerless Makeeda, or the statuesque and voluptuous Monica Jackson, Marni's mom, whom Laura had been happily and vigorously screwing lately. Sara was short, a little thick around the middle, with a large though very shapely ass, and a rather plain face which nevertheless was capable of a wide range of zany expressions, and was serenely lovely in repose, or when locked in the ecstatic wince of a sharp orgasm. And of course she had breasts that Laura daydreamed about, beautiful gourd-shaped globes with very large and puffy black areolas. She could suck them for hours—Sara clearly loved it too—and then come unbelievably with one in her mouth.

Like most women, Sara was well aware of her flaws. But she was quite willing to play along. She pirouetted. "You think so? What about these thunder thighs? And the booty that makes the Kardashians quiver with envy?" She gave Laura a salacious thrust with her large bottom. "Oomph!"

Laura grabbed her again. "If I suck one of your nipples, I'll come," she whispered into Sara's ear, giving voice to her thoughts.

"Ooohhh," Sara squealed, again twisting away, forming a little tray with the flattened backs of the fingers of both hands under her splendid breasts. "And I can hear them calling, too. 'Suck me . . . suck me! Laura's gonna suck meeeee!'"

Oh god, I can't take much more of this, Laura thought, feeling her hot blood race and throb. I love this woman and want to fuck her so much. Sara seemed to feel the same way. They kissed in a heated, almost dangerous, collision, their teeth clanking painfully. Sara pulled back, giggling.

"You know, the dentist just left with his wife for a week in Florida. He ain't here to repair the damage from us knocking each other's teeth out."

Laura nipped her earlobe playfully. "If we can't go to your place, maybe we can do it here."

"You're kidding."

Laura shook her head. "Lock the doors." She gestured toward the waiting room. "There's a sofa out there."

Sara made an excruciatingly comical face. "Oh right. Are you out of your mind! Let's fuck where I work. Haven't you heard that you don't shit where you eat?"

"Who's talking about shit?" She ran her lips up and down Sara's short neck and squeezed her delectable firm breasts through her clothes. "I want to fuck you."

Sara laughed and squirmed away. "And I want you to. But . . . here?"

"Okay, you think of a better idea."

Sara melted a little. After all, Laura thought, they did have a history. By now they had spent years fucking each other. At first frequently, as they had had a heated intimate union, with lots of insatiable romping. Later, after they had broken up, more sporadically, which if anything made their couplings even hotter, since not only did absence make the heart grow fonder (and the pussy hungrier, Laura reasoned), but both were cheating on subsequent lovers, Laura on Makeeda, Sara on Darlene. A little seasoning of guilt never failed to get the hot juices running.

Sara too seemed reluctant to relinquish this opportunity. She acquiesced. "Let me at least lock the doors."

Laura waited patiently by Sara's desk while Sara locked both the main entry door from the hall to the waiting room, and the back office door, which also exited to the hallway. She returned with the keys, deposited them in her desk drawer, then took Laura's hand, tugging her in the direction of the dentist's own office, in the rear of the complex. "Not out there in the waiting room," she murmured to Laura. "I think I would feel too inhibited out there. Anyway, somebody passing in the corridor outside might hear us. You make me yelp sometimes."

Laura grinned. "I know. I can't wait to make you squeal and moan."

Sara gave her a disapproving smirk. "This is only because of Mama. I mean, doing it here. It's so risky. It makes me so nervous . . . god, I might not even be able to come."

"Oh, yes you will!" Laura said brightly, pulling her closer as they entered the dentist's office and squeezing her ass cheeks through her skirt with both hands. "Mmmm, give me that beautiful ass."

Sara laughed and swatted her hands away. "You're a maniac. You were never this way when we were together. So shamelessly horny."

"Oh yes I was. You just forget. I couldn't get enough of this hot body."

Inside the dentist's private office there were book cases, and a desk, diplomas and posters picturing dental procedures on the walls, and a long sofa against one wall. Laura grinned in appreciation. Sara knew what she was doing. She might be a little nervous about having sex here, but she knew which room was best for it. "He won't come back?" she asked as Sara led her to the sofa.

Sara shook her head. "I told you, he went to Boca with his wife for a convention." She made a comical face. "Imagine what it's like when three thousand dentists get together for the week. Yick."

They sat together on the long sofa. "This will do just fine," Laura said, reaching for Sara, embracing her, kissing her smooth neck up and down, sucking her earlobe.

"It's extra long because he likes to take naps in the middle of the day. He's, like, six three or six four." Sara laughed softly. "If we fuck here, I'll never be able to look at it again without smiling."

"If I have my way, you'll probably break into song each time you see it," Laura teased, trying to unbutton Sara's blouse while she kissed her neck.

"Not so fast," Sara demurred, again pushing her hands away. "We don't have to hurry. Kiss me a little. You know how you love these fat nigga bubble lips."

"Don't say that," Laura frowned. "I love your lips. So soft and pillowy and sensual. The first time I saw you, sitting out there in the front office, I just tingled all over with the urge to kiss these fantastic lips."

They kissed slowly and emotionally. "You just a hot white girl with jungle fever," Sara joked when they paused for a moment, lapsing into a touch of ebonics, which she rarely did.

"Fever for you," Laura pouted. "You know I love you."

"Don't say that . . . when it isn't true."

"Of course it's true."

"What about the singer? Your wife." Sara pointed at the gold band on Laura's finger.

Laura could not conceal an unfortunate blush. She tried to cover it up by kissing Sara quickly and hungrily under her jaw and along her cheek and over to her lips again. "You know things happen. It doesn't mean my heart doesn't still go ping! when I see you."

"It's yo little pink pussy going ping, girl. 'I think I'd like to stick my fist up that short girl's black pussy. If I can wedge my hand between those thunder thighs.'"

"Will you quit it!" Laura cried out, almost hysterically, she realized from hearing the upward keening sound of her own voice. "You're being mean! You know I love you, you *know* what I mean!"

Sara softened. "I know what you mean," she said quietly. "I'm sorry for teasing you." She made a disgusted face. "But you did leave me for her."

Laura pouted. "I did not. We drifted apart. How many times do I have to tell you that?"

In reply Sara began unbuttoning her own blouse, the usual office-style crisp white shirt, so striking against her smooth dark brown skin, more and more of which was quickly coming into view. "I think you better fuck me before we both get so emotional that we can't go on."

Laura knew exactly what she was talking about. Some things were better left unsaid, especially since they still had this heated physical need for each other. The presence of Darlene and Makeeda in their lives shouldn't be allowed to get in the way of this crazy urge. Sara already had her own blouse unbuttoned all the way down the front, having tugged the bottom free of her skirt. Laura's hands were inside the loose fabric, on her warm flesh. Her fingers were behind Sara's back, searching for her bra clasp.

Sara giggled softly and kissed her neck. "Oooohhh, I think I'm gonna get sucked."

Laura was kissing her cleavage, and the bulging tops of her breasts, still frantically trying to undo the bra clasp. "You are if I can ever get this damned thing undone."

"You can't suck me until I can suck you too," Sara panted, hurriedly unbuttoning Laura's blouse too, which fastened up the back. All this feverish scrambling and fussing lasted only a few more seconds, and then they were both naked from the waist up.

They could not wait to embrace until they got the rest of their clothes off, and so they literally fell on each other with sharp, hungry passion. I have not felt her body for six months! Laura realized as she ran her hands all over Sara's smooth, warm flesh, and sucked it everywhere, neck, collar bones, shoulders. Her hands held and squeezed Sara's firm breasts, and Sara's held hers, and they tried to devour each other. Laura could hear the sucking sounds they both made, and their soft panting, which aroused her to an almost frantic pitch.

"God . . . I miss you so much!" she confessed in a soft whisper.

"Don't adore me, Laura," Sara panted, as she often had before. "Just get on with it. You're making me so wet!"

She sucked one of Sara's large, dark, bulbous nipples into her mouth before Sara could continue, sucking it in deep, with voracious passion. Sometimes Sara would yelp or squeal when Laura inadvertently sucked her amazing nipples this hard, but this time she only made a happy, guttural little groan, and her eyes rolled up.

"Unnmmgg! Oh . . . shit . . . Laura, that feels good! Do it harder!"

Laura held Sara's firm, gourd-shaped breast in both hands and literally devoured her saliva-wet, shiny nipple, tongue-lashing it, playfully tugging it with her teeth, sucking it again, long, passionate gulps.

"Oh! Oh! Oh!" Sara whimpered, looking down at her wet breast disappearing into Laura's hungry mouth. "God . . . unnngghh . . . oh! Do the other one!" she gasped to Laura, after a few seconds of this. Then smiled devilishly. "It's getting jealous."

Laura very wetly sucked Sara's other nipple the same way until both of them were gripped by a lust frenzy. "You're a glutton for titty sucking," Laura teased her, mauling the woman's exquisite breasts with her mouth and fingers.

"I know!" Sara giggled. "Darlene won't suck me the way you do."

"Mmmm . . . like this?"

"Auunngghhh! Oh . . . fuck. Yes!"

"And this?"

"Oh god! I'm going to come if you keep it up. Did you bring a strap-on?"

Laura shook her head. "I thought we'd probably go to your place. As I recall, you guys have two or three."

"One, cuckoo bird," Sara frowned. "Who needs more than one?"

She looked down at her shiny wet breasts and erect nipples and Laura's fingers squeezing them, and her eyes rolled up again. "I guess you'll have to do me with your hand. Quick. I'm dying for it. You really know how to make a girl horny."

"I want to fuck you with my pussy." Laura had deep cravings to feel their wet cunts grinding together, making them groan and come in the same shocking spasm.

But Sara shook her head. "I need to be fucked. You started it. Now . . . I need it."

Laura kissed her neck, her throat, her collar bones, on the way back down to her luscious naked breasts, still streaked with tiny, silvery trails of Laura's own saliva. "Does my honey want the Evil Fist? Does she want to get rammed until she squeals and screams?"

"Don't make me scream here, Laura," Sara said calmly as she slipped out of her skirt and panties. She nodded at Laura to do the same. "I'm not going ahead if you're not nakee too."

Laura raced to get out of the rest of her clothes. Somehow fucking here in the dentist's office, on the very sofa where he grabbed his afternoon cat naps, was wildly exciting. And being naked with Sara was also scintillating and dangerous and fiercely erotic. They might not be long-term partners any more, but nothing could squelch this fiery hunger they had for fucking. True, they had both tried to deny it. But when they met like this, twice a year, they could hardly wait to rip off their clothes and fuck in a blazing fury of need. It seemed to come over Sara at the same instant, that they were both plunged into this crazy biannual lust storm. She was sucking Laura's nipples now herself so insistently and passionately that Laura could barely wriggle out of her skirt and panties.

But finally they were both naked. They kissed with scorching hunger. "God . . . I didn't realize how much I missed this," Sara panted against Laura's neck, her hand sliding down to Laura's wet, oozing crotch.

Laura's fingers had already found Sara's pussy, which was warm and soupy and slippery, a small, plump, meaty pussy she had feasted on gloriously for years now. She scissored Sara's fat little clit between her forefinger and middle finger and rubbed it hard.

"Ahhnngg! Oh!" Sara gasped.

"Lie back." Laura eased her onto her back on the sofa cushions. "Do you want something to bite down on? Because I *am* going to make you scream."

"Oh . . . Laura . . . unngghh! You better not! Somebody will hear us!"

Laura realized it was possible . . . but doubtful. They were about thirty or so yards from the outside corridor, with several closed doors intervening. It was after five-thirty by now, and so patients would have stopped showing up for appointments. And last of all, people expected to hear yelps and screams from a dentist's office anyway, didn't they?

"We'll tell them I'm drilling you," she teased. "For a filling!"

She squeezed Sara's luscious breasts again with both hands, then began sucking her big bulbous nipples again too. She realized that the only thing they really had to fear was Darlene, Sara's dental hygienist lover who worked in the same building, showing up unexpectedly while they were locked in a sweet agony of orgasmic bliss. But the outer doors were locked.

"Where's Darlene these days?" she asked Sara, in an oblique, off-hand manner, while moving her mouth from one thick wet nipple to the other.

Sara couldn't suppress a giggle. "Her mother's in town too, if you can believe it. Don't worry, she won't barge in on us. She couldn't get in anyway. I locked the doors, remember?"

"Mmmm . . . music to my ears," Laura purred, on her way south, kissing Sara's naked body below her breasts, kissing her smooth stomach, her inner thighs, quickly approaching her blossoming pussy, which was all hot pink and slick and glimmering with juice.

Sara's pussy ring, which had so startled Laura years ago when she had done this for the first time, was no longer there of course, since Darlene had insisted she remove it; Laura could never figure why. Apparently to Darlene it signified that Sara was either a fan of twisted adornments and weird piercings, or she was an ungovernable lust maniac who loved having her nether regions stimulated continuously by a little dangling piece of metal. Either way, Laura surmised, it represented danger and had to be removed.

"I miss your pussy ring," she said softly as her lips approached the fragrant, festering slit of Sara's sweet, puckering pussy.

"I do too," Sara half-gasped, as Laura's tongue slipped between her pussy lips and into the honey pot. "Oh! Oh . . . that feels good!" She let Laura lick her for a minute or two, then asked: "Why do you miss it?"

Without skipping a beat, Laura murmured, into this plump, wet pussy she was passionately licking, "I just hate that cunt having control over you."

"Unh!" Sara gasped, unable to stop herself. "You . . . oh god, Laura, shoot, that feels so good! You shouldn't . . . unhh! . . . say that about her. Don't call her that."

Laura refrained from saying anything else but slipped two fingers into the tight, slippery crease and began to fuck her with them, while still aggressively licking her clit. Sara gave in to the rhythm and began churning her hips in answer to Laura's thrusts.

This went on for some time. Though both of them were seriously aroused now, they also wanted it to last, and through long experience, were quite capable of stretching it out. If Sara drew too close to a climax, Laura would slow the pace, and distract her from the final spasm by kissing the smooth, velvety flesh of her inner thighs, or her flat rising and falling belly, before returning to her engorged clit. Sara moaned and twisted, and squeezed her own breasts and pinched and pulled her own nipples, but she knew what Laura was doing and let her body slacken and relax a little in preparation for another crescendo.

"Oh god . . . I need you to fuck me hard," she finally panted to Laura, unable to endure any more delay. "Please . . ."

"I still want to fuck you with my pussy," Laura panted, trying to maneuver their bodies so that she could press her own crotch against Sara's.

She was close, forcing Sara onto her back, straddling one of her thighs, inching closer, when Sara suddenly fought back, pushing Laura down, insisting. "Please. Please . . . Laura . . . unhhh! Oh . . . god! I want it. Fuck me with your hand. I'm so close! You're going to make me come!"

I'm sure going to give it a shot, Laura thought, giving in to Sara's acute need, sliding back down between her yawning thighs and slipping three fingers back up into her warm, tight, well-lubricated slit.

"Unngghh!" Sara groaned, her eyes rolling up. She began to churn her pelvis and clench her hands into fists as Laura ratcheted up the rhythm, slipping her fourth finger, then her thumb, into the wedge that was invading Sara's hot pussy. "Mnnggawwong!" Sara suddenly groaned as Laura's entire hand slid up into her cunt. "Oh god!"

"Yes . . . honey! Yes . . . honey . . ." Laura murmured to her, twisting her hand, feeling her knuckles rub against the spongy inner sleeve of Sara's tight slit.

There was something about fist-fucking, they both knew. It might not be that way with everybody, but with a special person—and Sara certainly was special, she and Laura having been lovers long before their currently involvements—there could be, when you had nearly half your arm shoved halfway up a woman's body, a kind of solemn intimacy that no other act could match. Followed by, more often than not, a stupendous orgasm, a ripping, roaring, wrenching kind that left one awed and melting with love and the other a totally devastated wreck of coruscating and crushing bliss. It made some, like Bonnie—and maybe it was beginning to make Sara—a slave to this sweet practice, so that only a killer, pulverizing climax brought on by the fist could leave them completely satiated.

At any rate, Sara was now going almost wilder than Laura had ever seen her before as she churned her pussy down into Laura's upthrusting hand, squeezing her thighs tight on Laura's forearm, her eyes rolling up, her face contorted by sex need, and her groans becoming louder, punctuated by fierce little grunts as she drew nearer and nearer to the wrenching climax she sought. Laura helped her every inch of the way, plunging her hand into the tight, greasy sleeve of Sara's pussy, and leaning forward to suck her delectable, swollen, gleaming black nipples with the passionate thirst she always had for them.

She knew they were far from the hallway; she knew it was after five; she knew several doors and walls intervened between them and whatever passersby might be in the corridors. But she also knew there was about to be a stupendous sexual conflagration here, and that Sara was clearly beyond the point of caring if she were overheard.

What to do? Cover Sara's mouth with one hand? Let up on the plunging, thrusting motion of the other hand that was bringing them ever closer to the explosion?

"Unnhh! Mnnggowwnngg! Oh shit! Unghh! Oh shit . . . Laura! Ohhh! Do it HARD!"

Sara settled the whole thing for both of them. She suddenly reached down with both hands, quickly gripping Laura's wrist and forearm where it protruded from her crammed pussy, and with a fierce groan began to fuck herself on Laura's hand and arm in wild abandon, surging and groaning and pumping and . . . suddenly coming in a wild spasm of shrieks and convulsions.

"ANNGGMMNNGGHHIIIEEE!" she cried out, unable to stop the screams of pleasure from ripping and tearing out of her throat. Laura was seconds late getting her hand over Sara's mouth, and even then she could only partially prevent the escape of the following shrieks and roars. "Mmmnngghiiieeee! Ohhhh! AAUUWWONNGGG!"

Sara flipped and twisted under her on the sofa, flexing and shuddering as each new piercing wave of her climax wrenched her delectable naked body. Since her loudest screams quickly faded, to be replaced by softer whimpering and gasping as the strongest spasms of her orgasm softened into a succession of milder jolts, Laura hardly bothered trying to muffle them.

"Ooooohhhhhh!" Sara mewled, gnawing her lower lip, her face still half-torn by the shocking aftermath of this amazing climax. "Oh . . . shit . . . oh shit!" she gasped softly as aftershocks gripped her, her eyes fluttering open to look down at Laura's arm still protruding from her impaled pussy. Minutes seemed to go by as she slowly regained her senses and her breath. "Oh shit, Laura . . . nobody ever fucked me that hard. Not even you." She blinked, still stunned, but not so stunned as to keep from making a little joke. "God, you got to see my O Face full on, didn't you."

"Oh, come on, now," Laura demurred, kissing her neck and shoulders and running her free hand over Sara's lovely breasts, her nipples still damp with Laura's saliva. "You did all that yourself. I just supplied the hand. And your O face, as you call it, is beautiful."

Sara smiled wanly, glancing down. "Speaking of. Could you take it out now? It feels as big and hard as a baseball bat."

She winced as Laura withdrew her wet hand slowly. Laura leaned close and kissed her with deep emotion as her hand came out of Sara's clinging pussy. The aura of deep intimacy that surrounded this sexual act for them still wreathed their bodies as they kissed. "I lov—" Laura began, but Sara put one finger to her lips, shaking her head.

"Don't say it." She kissed Laura's nose. "We both know it. We don't have to say it."

Laura nodded, resigned. Sara was right. I love her in a special way. She knows it. She loves me too. We both know it. We'll have to live with that.

"I hope the security guards didn't send for the fire department," she whispered against Sara's silky cheek. Her wet hand brushed Sara's thigh, and Sara grimaced.

"Eewww! You're all wet."

Laura playfully licked her palm. "Wet with you," she smiled.

Sara pushed her away and jumped to her feet, a movement that made her luscious breasts bounce alluringly and that made Laura want to devour them all over again. Still stark naked, she went to the door that led from the dentist's office back into the treatment rooms. "Hold on, I'll get a towel."

Moments later she returned with a small stack of white cotton towels. "Here, wipe your hand off. And quit looking at my boobs as if they were T-bone steaks."

Laura cleaned her hand with a towel. "They are much better looking than T-bone steaks. Anyway, I don't go that much for meat."

"Ha! That's obviously a lie. I happen to know you go for dark meat in the worst way."

Laura made a face and shrugged. She cleaned off her hand, and Sara cuddled with her again on the sofa, nuzzling her neck for a little post-coital affection. Again they kissed with the aching love that had permeated their previous kiss. Then they dozed for a few minutes in the throbbing afterglow of sexual paradise. Finally, Sara perked up. "Well . . . I guess the fire department's not coming. They would've been here by now. They have like a five-minute response time or something. I'm a fire drill warden for this floor of the building. They get here quick, when it's just practicing."

"Ooohhh, I would love to see you in your little yellow plastic fire helmet. Buck naked, out there directing people to the stairs."

Sara pinched her. "It's very serious. I'm . . . responsible!"

"I know," Laura giggled. "But I'd want to grab you and fuck you."

"You want to do that anyway."

"I know."

Sara was warming up again. She began caressing and kissing Laura's naked body. "If they're not coming, we should get on with it. Your turn." She sucked Laura's nipples aggressively, until Laura began to moan softly, and squirm. "Oooo, Laura, you're all wetty wetty," she cooed as her fingers slipped up into Laura's soupy, tingling quim. She slid down a little between Laura's spreading thighs. "I think I'm gonna get me some of that. You know how I love Laura's pussy juice."

"You better . . . be . . . careful," Laura panted. "I might come right in your face."

Sara grinned up at her, already spreading Laura's cunt lips with her fingers. "Won't be the first time."

Laura tried to lie back and relax. Sara had eaten her pussy and brought her to thrilling, excruciating climaxes so many times in the past that she knew all she had to do was let nature take its course, enjoy it to the max, and come unbelievably, which, she told herself, was not going to be hard after the thrill moments ago of watching Sara nearly faint in the grip of a fierce fisting orgasm. Me too, she thought, with a tiny grin. I'm next.

"Ohhhhh . . . nnmmmm!" she twisted and moaned as Sara's clever tongue slid up into her wet pussy. "Oh . . . shit!"

Sara was smacking her lips with relish. "You don't like it?"

"Oh god, I love it! Do it faster!"

Sara rubbed the warm, buttery groove of Laura's blossoming cunt with two fingers while she teased and kissed Laura's clit at the same time, driving Laura crazy with need. She panted and writhed wildly.

Half of her wanted to be fist-fucked, the way she had moments ago fisted Sara into a hot seizure of happy, exuberant coming. She rarely felt that way, being more devoted to the giving end than the receiving one. But they were so relaxed and physically hungry for each other at this moment, she wanted, half of her wanted, to feel the same thing Sara had been feeling, the sensation of being filled and crammed and almost violently ploughed and inundated by sexual passion. And yet the other half of her wanted simply to give her body completely to Sara to use as she chose. She knew almost anything Sara attempted would make her climax only a few more seconds from now, and she was willing to surrender herself totally to the outcome.

Just fuck me and love me, she found herself chanting inwardly, to herself, over and over again. Fuck me and love me the way I love you. Please, Sara. "Awwonnggg!" she groaned, feeling the anticipatory spasms of a gigantic orgasm beginning to stir deep in her body.

Sara was still frenetically busy fucking her with two fingers while sucking her clit with those heavenly lips. Whether she knew Laura was about to come, or didn't, Laura soon ceased to care as a powerful wave of shattering orgasmic undulations began to wrack her quivering body.

"Annhh! Unnhhmmm! Oh! Unnggg! Oh . . . fuck . . . oh . . . honey!"

"Mmmm," Sara smiled, still sucking.

"AUUNGGGHH!" Laura exploded. Her body jackknifed violently in the air off the sofa, her thighs clenching together instinctively on Sara's head, her pelvis flipping and juddering wildly as the orgasm wrenched her. "Oh! Ohnnnngg! AAUUNNGGHH!" she cried out again.

Sara held on, but just barely. She began giggling and gurgling with laughter as the fierceness of Laura's climax became apparent, looping her arms around Laura's thighs and kissing Laura's exploding pussy with fresh ardor.

Laura was wrenched and hammered by it, but not so much that she too didn't bubble over with laughter at the epic release of sexual tension from her body, which soon collapsed into a long, slow, rippling swoon as minor aftershocks poured through her flesh. She grinned wanly down at Sara's face between her yawning thighs, and both of them nearly erupted in giggles again.

"We have to start doing this more than twice a year," she said, hearing her voice croak hoarsely. "I think we both store up too much in between."

Sara was ostentatiously licking Laura's pussy juices off her amazing lips as she scooted back up face to face with Laura. "I think you may be right. Thought I might have to call the Fire Department after all there for a minute. Just to get the EMTs here."

Laura embraced her, pulling Sara's whole naked body down on top of her. "Kiss me."

They kissed, wetly and lengthily. Then Sara nestled her head in Laura's neck, holding her, unwilling to move. "Sometimes, when I'm doing it with Darlene, I pretend she's you. Is that bad?"

Laura considered it. "I don't know. Do you think it is?"

"It makes me come harder. Isn't that awful?"

"I'm flattered. But you're probably not being fair to her. She loves you, after all."

"So do you."

"God, I do. You're right." Laura was embarrassed since she knew Sara was acutely aware of her deep love for and commitment to Makeeda.

But Sara was always quick to feel such vibrations. She turned her head and pecked Laura affectionately on her cheek. "Don't worry, I know you love her most." She nestled her head again in Laura's neck. "Anyway, it makes me feel a little guilty. I think we better fuck again while we've got the chance. We won't see each other for another six months."

Laura responded by writhing her naked body against Sara's suggestively, then fondling her exquisite pear-shaped breasts and thick protruding black nipples. "I think you are right," she smiled.

"I wish you'd brought a strap-on. I need to be rammed hard by you."

"Something tells me we already did that."

"I know," Sara laughed. "I'm such a slut. You bring out the slut in me, too. Darlene can't handle it."

"No more about Darlene, okay?" Laura slid down between her parting thighs and began licking her freshly moist pussy, parting the shiny black lips with her fingers.

"Oh!"

"Mmmmm, you like that."

"Yes! Oh! Unh!"

They had apparently talked enough and therefore submerged themselves in sex for several minutes, Laura licking and probing, Sara twisting and whimpering and growing progressively more and more overheated. Laura found herself remembering how they could do this for hours, back when they were together. She had spent more time simply enthralled in the sexual act, or acts, with Sara, it seemed, than with almost anyone else. Except Makeeda.

After a few minutes of making passionate love to this blossoming passion flower, she began to run her forefinger up and down in the tight crease between Sara's substantial buns, tickling the pinched little ring of her anus with her fingertip and feeling Sara's undulating body jerk and twitch at the exciting stimulation of her anal nerves. She also emitted a small, choked off yelp of surprise and pleasure.

"Mnnee! Ooohhh . . . wow! Yes!"

"You want that?" Laura panted, busy now sucking her nipples again, and biting her neck, her earlobe.

"Oh yes!"

Anal sex of any kind had come late to their game, since they had been so eager to try nearly every other way; but it had finally arrived. Sara was especially fond of the Double Penetrator, Laura's fiendishly exciting dual dildo strap-on that summoned epic orgasms almost every time. But she didn't have it with her today, of course. Fingers and tongues would have to do.

One thing they had never tried together was a rimjob, and Laura immediately thought of doing it now. She had had recent wild success doing it to Frankie, who nearly dissolved every time in acute sexual rapture as a result of it. Bringing Sara to a similar sexual spasm was an intriguing prospect, and she knew she could do it.

"Here . . . get on your knees," she prompted her, adjusting Sara's body so that she was on her hands and knees on the sofa, with her beautiful round ass uptilted to Laura's face.

It was a big one, especially for a short girl, but beautifully shaped. Sara loved to crack self-deprecating jokes about her 'huge ass,' or her 'bomber butt,' but Laura loved to pinch and squeeze and lick and bite it, each large resilient moon, and to make Sara squeal. Now she slowly pulled the large cheeks apart to reveal the puckered little aperture at the bottom of the deep, dark valley, inching her thumbs down into it to spread the little entryway more and more open, until she could get her tongue into it.

"Aiieeee!" Sara squealed, and tumbled into wild giggles. "Oh shit . . . Laura! That feels . . . sooooo good!"

Laura's tongue tip swept around the rim of Sara's anus, drawing another yelp from her.

"Mnneee! Oh . . . shit!" she again dissolved in giggles. "I hope you mean to do more than just tickle me!"

"Mmmm, I'm going to fuck you until you faint," Laura growled playfully, but also seriously, inserting two fingers now into the greasy warm slit of Sara's very wet and aroused pussy.

Knowing that Frankie nearly fainted in transports of rapture each time Laura tried it on her, she now began the process of bringing Sara to the same state. One thing was, however, clear. This was not a fast process. It wasn't a hot, rapid, urgent little procedure that culminated quickly in a fierce spasm of ecstasy. Instead, it might take ten minutes . . . or even twenty. It required patience and deliberation, but the reward was a shimmering supernova of a climax.

And so they settled quickly into the rhythm of it, Sara on her knees, her ass uptilted to Laura's serious ministrations, her soft panting and mewling a definite feedback clue to Laura of the slow, steady progress of her gentle probing. It wasn't hard for them since they had long experience of each other's body, leavened by a deep and unwavering affection that only grew deeper year after year, in spite of their other involvements. Deep into this act, many minutes into it, as Sara's breathing grew more rapid, and her whimpering more uncontrollable, her thighs flexing involuntarily, her anus periodically pinching Laura's tongue, she was unable to suppress her feelings.

"I . . . I love you, Laura," she gasped, now slowly swirling her beautiful round ass back and up into Laura's mouth and fingers, eyes closed, deep in concentration, biting her lower lip.

"I love you too, darling," Laura purred back.

"I . . . love this . . . but . . . I don't think I can come this way."

Laura never ceased her constant, gentle rhythm. Her tongue gently probed Sara's sensitive anus, while her two fingers slid slowly across the slippery, front inner wall of Sara's melting, oozing, overheated pussy. "Of course you can," she murmured. "You're almost there. I can feel it."

Sara fell silent again. More patient, relentless probing from Laura; more soft, clotted whimpering from Sara. Laura felt her shudder once or twice, not earth-shaking tremors but gentle rocking waves. Then, slowly, Sara began to gyrate her pelvis more rapidly. Her breathing increased too, becoming labored and scratchy.

"Oh . . .shit . . ." she suddenly gasped, in a slight panicked voice.

"Oh yes, honey. Oh . . . yes, honey," Laura responded, fucking her a little more quickly and roughly now, sensing that the finish was near.

Again Sara lapsed into silence, though her breathing still accelerated, and now became even more labored. Laura noticed she was digging her arms and elbows hard into the sofa cushions under them.

"Unnhhhh . . . unnnhhhh!" Sara groaned softly.

"Yes . . . honey."

"Oh . . . shit. Laur—"

Her body clenched. Laura could see the muscles in her thighs tighten fiercely. She felt a little spasm from Sara's pussy against her fingers, which were sunk and probing deeply inside it. And then . . . Sara burst. A hard, clenching spasm shook her tense body, followed by a loud, keening wail of shocking, piercing rapture.

"AnnnngghiiIIIEEEE! OOWWNNGGG! Unhhggg! Oh Jesus! Oh . . . fuck!"

And then she was completely robbed of breath by the intense shocks of a devastating orgasm, perhaps a more shattering one than any other Laura had seen her have. Sharp tremors gripped her collapsing body, followed by involuntary shaking, and tiny keening moans that came from deep in her chest.

"Ummmnnnggg! Ummnnnggg! Oh . . . oh god!"

It went on for a long time, long enough for Laura to worry about when it might end. Sara quivered, and twitched, and moaned softly. Finally, her entire pelvis gave one last twitch, and then her body went slack under Laura. The moaning ceased. She still panted and gasped but gave no other sign of life. At this point Laura, removing her fingers from Sara's wet pussy and her face from Sara's ass crack, swarmed over her prone body from behind, mashing her own naked breasts into Sara's back in the effort to kiss her and coax her back from this half-delirious trance of ecstasy the orgasm had caused.

"Oh honey . . . oh honey . . . are you all right?"

A harsh, explosive giggle escaped from deep in Sara's chest, half-muffled by the sofa cushion into which her face was stuffed. "Now . . . you ask me!" She lifted her head and turned her face up to Laura, crossing her eyes. "See what you did to me? You fucked me cross-eyed!"

Slowly, tenderly, they disentangled their bodies and embraced, stretching out along the full length of the dentist's sofa. Laura kissed her everywhere, still unable to get enough; filling her hands with the woman's marvelous naked breasts and squeezing them, sucking her neck.

"Hold on, girl," Sara giggled, twisting her neck and head away. "You just fucked me. You don't have to eat and swallow me too. Save some for Darlene, okay?"

"I hate her," Laura murmured. "I want you all to myself."

"Oooohhh!" Sara teased with a happy whoop. "I'm gonna tell the singer. Her hot wifey Laura done fucked her ex at the dentist's office while she was gone!"

"Are you my ex?" Laura feigned being abashed.

"Only one of them, you hot-pantsed little white tart," Sara pinched her thigh playfully. "You be fucking every sista on the block, if'n you get the chance." She loved dropping into ebonics when teasing Laura.

Though just a teasing remark, this was closer to the truth than Laura wanted to admit. A tear, a big tear, unsummoned, rolled down her cheek. Sara saw it and brushed it away with one finger.

"It's okay, I didn't mean it," she said. "You *are* my ex. If I think of you when I'm fucking with Darlene, which I do, you're my ex. I should be the one who's crying." She kissed Laura on the nose. "You horny white girls can cry on cue, can't you."

"Unnhhh . . ." Laura softly grunted. "Oh yes! Do that some more!"

While cuddling and kissing, Sara had slipped her sleek, meaty thigh between Laura's, and her thigh muscle pressed against Laura's wet pussy.

"You can feel that?"

"Not only can I feel it . . . you're going to make me come, if you keep it up. Ungghhh!"

"Ooohhh, then I *am*! I love to watch my Laura when she can't help herself and just spills over like a boiling pot. You are so pretty when you're groaning and screaming."

Laura, who loved watching a beautiful woman's O Face, as Sara called it, while she was climaxing had never had someone tell her they enjoyed watching hers. Somehow, this stirred her fire deep inside, and she began to feel a gathering tension in her pussy that could only lead to one thing.

"If you're going to do this . . . you have to do it hard," she panted to Sara, squeezing Sara's large thigh tightly between her own thighs and jamming her hot, wet pussy into the sleek muscle. "Really crunch it."

Sara made a funny face. "Something tells me you've done this before."

"Once or twice," Laura confessed. "Are you going to do it or not?"

"I wouldn't dream of depriving my baby of her satisfaction." She clenched her thigh and jammed it hard into Laura's oozing, throbbing pussy.

Laura's eyes rolled up. She groaned softly with hungry sexual sounds. "Ohhh shit! Oh . . . Jesus."

This in turn seemed to set Sara off. She immediately turned up the heat several notches, sensing how close Laura really was. "Better leave him out of it," she panted, turning serious, pushing Laura over onto her back and rising up, planting her palms on the sofa cushions for leverage and then ramming her thigh with fierce determination into Laura's aching pussy.

"Awwonnggg!" Laura howled, feeling sexual sparks careen through her tense body. Sara rarely fucked her hard, but she was doing it now. "Unggmmn! Oh!"

Sara's luscious, swaying breasts dangled over her face. "Go ahead and suck one, honey," she teased Laura. "I know how it makes you come. Suck me, baby. Suck . . . me . . . baby. Yes . . . yes!"

Laura hungrily sucked one of Sara's big chocolate cupcake nipples deep into her mouth and almost instantly felt the hot throbbing in her crotch begin to swell into an overwhelming bubble, about to burst. Sara ground the hard muscle of her thigh relentlessly into Laura's splayed and throbbing pussy, grunting softly from the effort, but crunching it home each time the way Laura had asked her to do.

"Unhh!" she grunted softly, her eyes rolling up as Laura sucked her large nipple roughly and aggressively.

"Awwonngg!" Laura gasped. Sara's wet nipple slipped from her mouth. "Shit . . . you're stronger than you look."

"Unhh! You bet. Unghh unhhh!"

'Awwoonng! Oh shit . . . just like that!" Laura groaned desperately, knowing she was going to come any instant now.

She began pumping back into each of Sara's thrusts. Wildly, her hands flew up and grabbed Sara's dangling breast, the other one she had not been sucking yet, and fed Sara's bulging black nipple into her mouth. She sucked it crazily and pumped vigorously against Sara's crunching thigh, feeling her whole lower body explode, and the liquid flame roar through her body as the climax finally wrenched her.

"Aaanngghhnnniiieeee!" she cried out, arching and straining, then shuddering wildly as a sharp orgasm gripped her. She clamped her thighs on Sara's and pumped for all she was worth, feeling one shock-wave after another roar through her arching body. "Anngghh! Angghh! Unh! Oh!"

She arched and shuddered so violently that she nearly dragged both of them off the sofa, but Sara grabbed the top of it in one hand to anchor them in place. She waited out Laura's lengthy spasming and groaning, finally, and playfully, mashing her saliva-damp breast back against Laura's mouth. "Suck some more," she teased softly. "You suck good. You almost make me want to have another one too."

Laura, still panting and half-stunned, smiled wanly up at her. "Are you going to let me get my breath or what? You little fuck demon. I didn't know you had it in you." She beamed. "Or I would've asked for that long ago."

Sara pulled gently away and looked down at her wet thigh muscle, slick with Laura's juices. "Eeuuwww! You all messy, girl!"

Laura kissed her gleaming dark brown shoulder. "I didn't hear you complaining when you were trying to mash my poor pussy into mush."

Sara reached for one of the white towels she had brought in earlier and placed on a table beside the sofa. She dried off her thigh. "It was kinda fun. You went like crazy. Maybe I should try it on Darlene."

"I'd be careful, if I were you. You have to be a stone cold masochist like me to really get off that way."

Sara made another in her rich repertoire of funny faces. "Guess next time you'll have to try it on *me*."

They were both reluctantly pulling on their clothes. "Next time," Laura said, "I'm bringing my strap-on so I can fuck your pretty brains out."

"Ooohhhh!" Sara shimmied her shoulders, giving Laura one last look at her marvelous naked breasts jiggling and swaying. "I can hardly wait! Let's go out front and put your appointment in the book right now!"

To be continued...

Here is a sample from another story you may enjoy:

Bonnie Chronicles

Compilation

EROTIC LESBIAN ROMANCE

MIRANDA MARS

WARNING:

This compilation contains lots of Oral Activities, Fisting, Strap-on Humping, and Thigh-Screwing. If Interracial Lesbian Romp offends you, do not read. Otherwise, enjoy!

The one thing that Laura first notices about Bonnie is her wall-of-fame butt, which whets her appetite and makes her want Bonnie so hard. So hard, in fact, that she goes through great lengths to have her.

And once she gets a taste of Bonnie, Laura is addicted. She can't get enough of this delicious black woman, even if it means sneaking in to Bonnie's apartment every time Laura's wife is not around.

But Laura is possessive that when she sees Bonnie with a butch-haired woman, she is consumed by jealousy. To make it worse, Bonnie tells her that they can't see each other anymore.

Bonnie's loyalty rests in Meredith, her new girlfriend, but Laura will not stop until she gets a taste of Bonnie again. Laura even persuades Bonnie to cheat on Meredith. But no matter how Bonnie tries to reject Laura's advances, Laura just knows how to set things in motion to get Bonnie.

If you enjoyed this sample then look for **<u>Bonnie Chronicles Compilation</u>**.

Also by this Author:

Deep Excavation

Chocolate Sandwich

Post-Game Specials

A Breach in the Preacher's Daughter

Deeply Detoured

The Rich Bitch Itch

"Hard" Competition

Little Rich Girls Go First

Superior Playmate

Spicing Up a Business Conference

Green Minds Lead to Colorful Results

Dirty Acquaintance

Menage a Trois

Provisional Test

Holiday Treat and Heat

Sex on the 46th Floor

Sneak, Peek and Squeak

Distance Leads to a Sexual Marathon

Confessions and Steamy Clinches

Screams of Pleasure

[Sweet Surrender](#)

[A Fine Day for Car-washing](#)

[A Reunion to Remember](#)

[Lustful Temptations](#)

[Love and Pain at the Dentist](#)

[Unwanted Visit](#)

[Sibling Rivalry](#)

[Her Undoing](#)

[Ashley's Sister Audrey](#)

[Infidelity Strikes](#)

[A New Love Nest](#)

[Sandwich Shop Seduction](#)

[Little Sex Bunny](#)

[A Secret Affair](#)

[The Girl of My Girl](#)

[Consumed By Jealousy](#)

[Erotic Explosion](#)

[Skylark . . . Have You Anything To Say To Me?](#)

[Laura Loves College Girls](#)

[Arthell Revisited](#)

[Arthell Loves To Kiss](#)

[Arthell Doubles Down](#)

There, I've Said It Again...

There's No One But You

There Is No Greater Love

Sex Frenzy

A Rising Star

Raging Desire

It Hurts So Good

I Remember You

Don't Adore Me, Just...

Bittersweet Reunion

And Sheena Makes Three...

Gail's Awakening

We'll Be Together Again

Taneesha Wants Some of That

"Some Say the World Will End in Fire... Some Say in Ice..."

Reckless Betrayal

Please Take Me Back, Baby!

Play Coquette

Pervert Devotion

My Little Yoga Darling

Icicles Can Melt

[Caught in the Act](#)

[Pull My Hair and Make Me Come!](#)

[The Emperor Wants Your Pussy!](#)

[Three on a Bed](#)

[No One Can Replace You](#)

[Lock Up the Dogs!](#)

[Not While She's Looking](#)

[Blindfold Me and Lick Me All Over](#)

[Do Me Up the Ass Please](#)

[Ride 'Em Cowgirl](#)

[I'm Going to Come So Fast](#)

[Gina Loves the Dick](#)

[Bathtub Sex With Frankie](#)

[Spanking Gina's Beautiful Black Ass](#)

[Finding Marni's G-Spot](#)

[Naked and Horny in the Woods](#)

[Marni Wants It Hard, Ashley Wants It Wet](#)

[Water My Ficus](#)

[Deshona Chronicles Compilation](#)

[Kissing Marni's Mom](#)

[Shagging Shamika's Aunt](#)

[Laura and Gail Chronicles](#)

Laura and Frankie Chronicles

Laura and Arthell Chronicles Compilation

Laura and Makeeda Chronicles Compilation

Bonnie Chronicles Compilation

About the Author

Miranda Mars lives with her cats and her exercise machines with her "special" friend in a suburb in San Francisco. Here is where she lavishly spends scribbling erotica for your, and her own, amusement.

She is especially attracted to dark-skinned women, and uses them as the lovers of the main characters in the stories she writes. She says they're just so hot! So dark-skinned women, BEWARE! :-)

Her stories are also surprisingly VERY ENTERTAINING for MEN!

From the Author

If you'd like to give me comments or suggestions to any of my books, feel free to shoot me an email at:
miranda_mars@awesomeauthors.org.

Check my page on Amazon and my blog for Updates and interesting info.

Author Central - http://amzn.to/14wSFHW
Author Blog - http://miranda-mars.awesomeauthors.org/

If you enjoyed any of my books then please share the love and click like on my books in Amazon.

If you write me a review and send me an email I will send you a free book, or many.
(Just know that these emails are filtered by my publisher.)

Good news is always welcome.

One Last Thing, For Kindle Readers...

When you turn the page, Kindle will give you the opportunity to rate this book and share your thoughts on Facebook and Twitter. If you enjoyed my writings, would you please take a few seconds to let your friends know about it? Because... when they enjoy they will be grateful to you and so will I.

Thank You!

Miranda Mars
Miranda_mars@awesomeauthors.org

5025965R00029

Printed in Germany
by Amazon Distribution
GmbH, Leipzig